To Barney and
with love
from Peng 2019 love

# Hervé
## Saves the Day

ISBN: 978-0-9928926-7-8

Published & printed by Capital Press Ltd, Canterbury, Kent CT3 4NH
www.capitalpress.co.uk

*Stephen would like to dedicate this book to Meme,*
*for keeping up with Hervé and all of his adventures.*

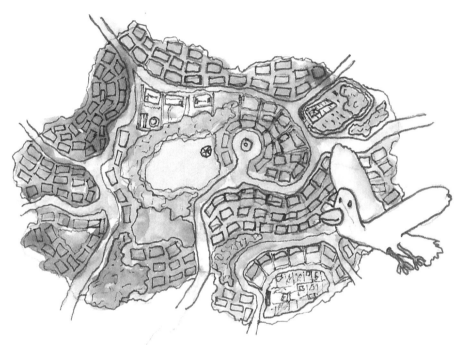

The little town of Boeuf-sur-Mer

Sleeps soundly in the midnight air,

Its streets are dim, its lights are out.

Is there anyone about?

No.. but… wait! A little spark

Of light shows up against the dark.

A peep through a window pane reveals

The fevered head of Monsieur Gilles.

Bent over figures, rows of facts,

Poor Monsieur Gilles divides, subtracts,

In desperation, multiplies,

But no matter how he tries

Monsieur Gilles has to confess,

His camp's accounts are in a mess.

He sighs and puts his books away.

'Tomorrow I must see Hervé'.

Hervé's aghast: 'Is this a joke?'

'No,' says Gilles, 'the campsite's broke,

The campers go to the other site

Where they can stay out late at night,

Dance at the disco or drink at the bar,

There's a hot pool and a bubbly spa.

Our simple campsite can't compete

The campers are voting with their feet.

A campsite that can't pay its way

Will have to close, I'm sad to say.

And Hervé, *mon brave,* this grieves me most

You will have to lose your post.

Now take this note down to the mayor

Ask him to pin it in the square'.

Hervé sets off with a heavy heart.

How was it he, the brave, the smart

Who'd ruled the camp with iron fist

At a stroke could be dismissed?

A lone tear trickles down his nose,

As into town poor Hervé goes.

Joseph tossing crêpes suzettes,

He stops in the market square to see
Everywhere activity:

The baker baking fresh baguettes,

The park attendant mowing grass,

12

The teacher frowning at her class.

Hervé watches enviously:

'They've all got jobs, except for me!'

He wanders idly past some shops

Towards the *mairie* and stops.

A bright red poster takes his eye

Informing every passer-by:

'Grand circus! Twenty-third of June!

First performance here, at noon'.

A circus! Hervés braincells whirr.

The worm of an idea begins to stir!

Monsieur Gilles sighs when he hears his scheme:

'Hervé, *mon vieux,* just a pipe dream!'

But Hervé's fired up and persists,

'Give me two weeks!' he insists.

'Two weeks to turn the camp around

And make its future outlook sound.'

Monsieur Gilles shrugs: 'Have it your way!

Two weeks but not another day!'

With a whisker whisk and a flick of his tail

Hervé is off on the campaign trail.

Reports come in that he's been seen

With the mayor, the priest and in between

Down at the local village school

At Joseph's bar and the swimming pool.

But if you ask him when and why

He's not telling and neither am I!

On the fourteenth night in the nick of time
(Remember Monsieur Gilles' deadline?)
Hervé creeps out, in disguise,
A muffler pulled up to his eyes,
Dark glasses to escape detection,
Pulling behind him a strange collection
Of brushes, hammers, screws and nails
And black and yellow paint in pails.

Hervé reaches Boeuf-sur-Mer,

Goes to the point in the village where

One road leads to the rival site

With its bars and spas and neon light.

Chuckling, Hervé blocks this way

With a large sign saying: *'Route barrée',*

Then, to prevent hesitation,

Pins up a new sign 'Deviation'

And paints arrows leading right

Back to Monsieur Gilles' campsite!

Next day a line of campers wait

Impatiently at Hervé's gate,

Full of righteous indignation

At the '*route barrée*' and the 'Deviation',

But what a vision greets their eyes!

Their mouths fall open in surprise!

And anger changes to delight:

A circus sprung up in the night!

In one spot the school band plays
A rather wobbly *Marseillaise,*
Over there, the majorettes
In red and yellow epaulettes
March in time behind the mayor,
Tossing his baton in the air.

With teeth fear-clenched and streaming locks

The priest flits by on a flying fox.

Then, wonder of wonders, perched up high
Etched against the morning sky
On a tightrope, pirouetting,
Hervé the cat (no safety netting!).

24

The campers watch with baited breath
As our hero toys with death.
He wobbles, wavers but survives
(A cat, remember, has nine lives!).
The watching campers cheer and cheer
They say to each other 'Let's stay here!

This campsite's far more exciting

Than ours, for all its neon lighting!'

They pitch their tents and so that night

There's not a spare place on the site.

'Hervé', says Gilles, 'how do you do it?'

Hervé shrugs. 'There's nothing to it.

But I have something to declare:

I never took your note to *monsieur le maire*

For though the camp's accounts were grim,

Its chances of survival, slim,

I still felt we could save the site

And, as usual, I was right!'

*Fin.*

If you liked this story there are three other Hervé adventures to look out for

Now if your steps should chance to stray
Into Boeuf-sur- Mer one day,
On every twenty-third of June
In the village square at noon
You'll find a circus and a fête
In honour of Hervé the Great!